AEROPLANES

George Ivanoff

Contents

What Is an Aeroplane?

An aeroplane is an aircraft that transports people and objects. There are three important things that make an aircraft an aeroplane: it flies, it has wings that do not move and it has an **engine**.

A helicopter has an engine, but no wings.
A glider has wings, but no engine.
Only an aeroplane has both.

a helicopter

Most aeroplanes have two wings
– one on either side of the body.

Some aeroplanes have four wings – two on either side.
These are called "biplanes".

a glider

Propeller Engines

A plane with two propellers prepares to take off.

Some aeroplanes use propeller engines.
A propeller is a type of fan.
In a car, the engine makes the wheels go round.
The wheels make the car move.
In an aeroplane with a propeller, the engine makes the propellers go round. The propellers make the aeroplane move.

Some aeroplanes have only one propeller,
which is at the front of the machine.

Other aeroplanes have two propellers – one on each wing.
And some aeroplanes have even more propellers.

Jet Engines

Some aeroplanes use jet engines.

A jet engine works in three steps:

1. A fan sucks cold air into the front of the engine.
2. A **combustor** mixes the air with burning **fuel**.
3. A nozzle then blasts the hot air out the back of the engine.

The hot air blasted out the back of the engine pushes the aeroplane forwards.

How a Jet Engine Works

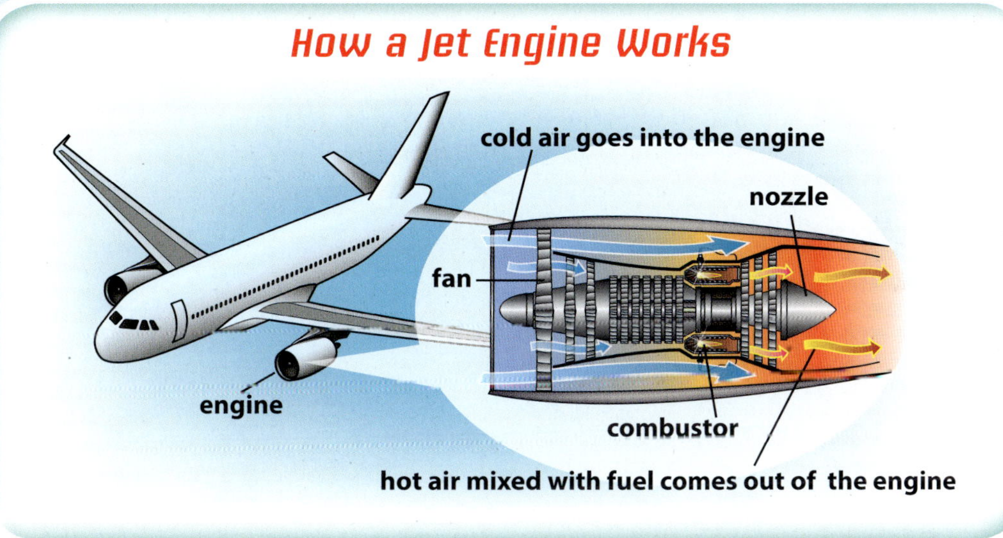

Aeroplanes with jet engines are now more common than aeroplanes with propeller engines. An aeroplane powered by a jet engine can fly faster than one with propellers.

The First Aeroplane

The first aeroplane was built in 1903,
by two American brothers called Wilbur and Orville Wright.

On 17 December 1903, Orville made the first flight
in an aeroplane called the *Flyer I.*
The flight lasted 12 seconds.
The aeroplane flew a distance of 37 metres.

The Wright brothers made many test flights
each time they changed the design of their aeroplane.

In 1904, the brothers built the *Flyer II*
and in 1905 they built the *Flyer III.*

With each new aeroplane, they were able to fly
for much longer periods of time.
On 5 October 1905, the *Flyer III* flew
for 39 minutes and 23 seconds.

Think and Talk About ...

The Wright brothers began flying with gliders before moving on to aeroplanes.

Orville (left) and Wilbur (right) Wright

Orville Wright makes the first flight in *Flyer I* while Wilbur watches on.

Across the Water

Louis Blériot flies his plane, *Blériot XI*, across the English Channel in 1909.

In 1908, an English newspaper, the *Daily Mail*, offered a prize of 1000 pounds to the first person to fly an aeroplane across the English Channel. The English Channel is the body of water between England and France. The French inventor, Louis Blériot, won the prize. On 25 July 1909, he flew across the channel in the *Blériot XI*. The flight took 36 minutes.

In 1927, American pilot Charles Lindbergh made the first non-stop flight across the Atlantic Ocean. He flew from New York to Paris. His aeroplane was called the *Spirit of St Louis*.

Charles Lindbergh and his aeroplane

American pilot Amelia Earhart was the first woman to fly solo across the Atlantic Ocean. She made the flight in 1932, five years after Charles Lindbergh.

Amelia Earhart flew from Newfoundland, Canada, to Northern Ireland on her first flight across the Atlantic.

Faster than Sound

Chuck Yeager and his aeroplane, the Bell X-1

The first aeroplane to travel faster than the speed of sound was the Bell X-1, in 1947. The Bell X-1 travelled at 312 metres per second.
It was flown by pilot Chuck Yeager, in America.

Since 1947, aeroplanes have become faster and faster. Aeroplanes that can travel faster than the speed of sound are called **supersonic**.

This is an artist's impression of the Lockheed SR-71.

Think and Talk About …

The world record for the fastest jet aeroplane is held by the Lockheed SR-71 "Blackbird", which flew at the speed of 3530 kilometres an hour. This record was set in 1976.

Aeroplanes in War

Aeroplanes changed the way wars were fought.
They took the fighting to the skies.
Aeroplanes were first used for war between Italy and Turkey, in 1911–1912.

Manfred von Richthofen's aeroplane was bright red.

During World War I (1914–1918),
fighter aeroplanes were built.
These aeroplanes had machine guns built into them.
People fighting on different sides used these aeroplanes
to shoot at each other in the sky.

Think and Talk About ...

The most famous World War I fighter pilot was Manfred von Richthofen, from Germany. He was known as the Red Baron. He shot down 80 aeroplanes.

In World War II (1939–1945), fighter aeroplanes became even more **advanced**, as jet fighters were built. Jet fighters are aeroplanes powered by jet engines that are used in war.

The first jet fighter to be used during the war was the German Messerschmitt Me 262.

The Messerschmitt Me 262 was first used in battle in 1944.

A Harrier "Jump Jet" takes off vertically.

Jet aeroplanes are now in every **air force**.

The British Harrier "Jump Jet" is one of the most famous jet fighter aeroplanes.

It has jets that point down so it can take off straight up into the air, without needing a runway.

Aeroplanes to the Rescue

Aeroplanes are used to save lives.
The Royal Flying Doctor Service of Australia was set up in 1928. Doctors use aeroplanes to visit patients who live in places a long way from towns. The service is still used today and is very important for people living in the **outback**.

The Royal Flying Doctor Service helps people in remote regions of Australia.

The Royal Flying Doctor Service uses aeroplanes as air ambulances. People living in **remote** places who have a medical emergency can be taken to the nearest hospital in these special aeroplanes. There is medical equipment on board an air ambulance, just like any other ambulance.

A firefighting plane drops water on a fire.

Special aeroplanes are used to help put out fires. The aeroplanes drop chemicals and water from large tanks onto the fire. This helps the firefighters on the ground.

Passenger Flights

A passenger aeroplane lands in Berlin, in 1948.

In the 1930s, flying became popular all around the world.
Larger aeroplanes were built to carry more **passengers**.
The Douglas DC-3, built in America in 1935,
was the first passenger aeroplane.
This aeroplane could carry 24 passengers.
People paid money to travel on this aeroplane.

The first passenger jet aeroplane was the de Havilland Comet.
It began flying in 1949 and it carried 36 passengers. Its first flight was from London, England, to Johannesburg, South Africa.

Passenger aeroplanes became bigger and bigger, as more people wanted to travel. The first "jumbo" jet aeroplane started flying in 1970. It was the Boeing 747 and it could carry 350 people. Now, thousands of people travel by aeroplane every day.

Think and Talk About ...

The world's largest passenger aeroplane can carry 525 passengers. It is a double-decker plane, called the Airbus A380. It began flying in 2005.

Today, it is difficult to understand what travel must have been like before aeroplanes were invented. Now, these amazing aircrafts are used to move people very quickly within their own countries and to places all around the world.

The *Dreamliner*

The Boeing 787, or *Dreamliner*, is a type of passenger jet aeroplane. It was first tested in 2009, and began flying with passengers in 2011. The *Dreamliner* can carry up to 335 passengers.

A Boeing 787 comes in to land.

The aeroplane was named the *Dreamliner* after a public naming competition. People from 160 countries were invited to vote for the name they liked best.

Think and Talk About …

Other names that were considered before *Dreamliner* was chosen included *eLiner*, *Global Cruiser* and *Stratoclimber*.

The *Dreamliner* is different from a lot of other passenger jet aeroplanes.
It does not use as much fuel
as other large passenger jet aeroplanes.
This is mainly because it is made from lighter materials.

The *Dreamliner* is not as loud as other jet aeroplanes.
It has been built with new **technology** that reduces the engine noise.

The *Dreamliner* is a very popular type of aircraft because of these things.

A crowd gathers to see a Boeing 787 at an airshow.

Glossary

advanced (*adjective*)	far on or ahead in progress
air force (*noun*)	a group of aircraft that a country uses for fighting in the air
combustor (*noun*)	the part of the engine where fuel is burnt
engine (*noun*)	a machine that makes things move
fuel (*noun*)	something that is burned to make heat or power
outback (*noun*)	land in Australia that is very far from cities and towns
passengers (*noun*)	people travelling in a vehicle
remote (*adjective*)	far from other people and towns
supersonic (*adjective*)	faster than the speed of sound
technology (*noun*)	the use of science in solving problems

Index